U0007187

Witty, Clever, Wisdom, Inspirational Sayings of

Oscar Wilde

人生太重要，
重要到不該嚴肅論之。
王爾德妙語錄

奧斯卡‧王爾德 —— 著
張家綺 —— 譯

Contents

「在我遭受辱罵時，
我知道我已觸及點點繁星。」——

oscar wilde.

愛爾蘭作家奧斯卡‧王爾德在一八五四年出生於一個家世卓越的都柏林家庭。他的父親是外科醫生，母親則是詩人與作家。童年時的王爾德在家中自學，受德國與法國家教教導，因此德語與法語皆流利。他在一八七四年在牛津大學就讀時，受到維多利亞時期的藝評家拉斯金 (John Ruskin) 的審美觀念和前拉斐爾派 (Pre-Raphaelite Brotherhood) 作品影響，奠定了日後成為唯美主義先鋒作家的方向。年輕的王爾德在出版首本《詩集》後便前往倫敦發展，雖然他當時沒有得過任何文學獎項，但奇特打扮和談吐機智的形象也讓他在倫敦社交界開始嶄露頭角。

一八八〇年，此時的王爾德已經打進倫敦社交圈。他的第一齣劇作《薇拉》在這一年完成，不過沒有得到迴響，最後也未在倫敦上演。一八八二年，已成名的王爾德受邀前往美國進行巡迴講座；他在進入美國海關時曾說：「我沒有什麼東西要申報，除了我的天才。」回國兩年後，他與在都柏林劇院相識的律師之女康斯坦絲‧勞埃德（Constance Lloyd）戀愛成婚，兩個兒子席瑞爾（Cyril）與維維恩（Vyvyan）也分別在一八八五與隔年相繼出生。（席瑞爾在一九一五年一次大戰期間參戰，遭德軍射殺身亡，英年早逝，而維維恩日後則成為作家及翻譯家。）

一八八七年，王爾德成為《婦女世界》（The Woman's World）雜誌的總編輯，並在雜誌上發表創作，以其立意新穎的觀點和獨特的文風聞名。次年五月，短篇故事集《快樂王子》出版。一八九〇年，原於報上連載的《格雷的畫像》奠定了他頹廢藝術家的地位。王爾德在這部長篇小說中，以豐富的想像和饒富哲理的優美語言，藉由奇特的情節發展揭露英國上流社會的道德沉淪和空虛；在這個善與惡交織、美與醜對立，靈魂從墮敗到毀滅的悲劇故事中，他完整闡述出自己對藝術和人生的觀點。這部唯一的長篇小說作品雖讓他贏得讚譽，但他的戲劇作品更是廣受歡迎。

王爾德劇作對話中的語言，是他在戲劇創作上的特別傑出之處。劇中詼諧的對話揭示了當時英國上流社會的迂腐與荒謬，許多名言警句甚至是從微不足道的小角色或

是負面人物口中說出，更添其中的深長意味，而且當中詞彙無不值得觀者推敲細賞。他擅長巧對王爾德來說，矛盾和對照修辭能充分表現他獨有的思考方式和語言風格。他擅長巧妙利用語意相反或對立的詞句表達自己複雜的思想和感情，或闡述某種意味深長的哲理，揭示人的複雜心理矛盾和人生哲理，同時也讓語言更顯流暢、豐富、趣味，角色個性和本質也因而更顯鮮明。

　　　·　　　·　　　·

　　一八九五年，在王爾德事業如日當空之際，昆斯伯理侯爵 (Marquess of Queensberry) 發現兒子道格拉斯 (Lord Alfred Douglas) 竟與他交往長達四年，因而對王爾德提告。由於昆斯伯理侯爵與道格拉斯這對父子關係長期不睦，道格拉斯因而要求王爾德上訴反擊他父親，控告侯爵毀謗。結果王爾德敗訴，反被控告「曾與男性發生有違風化的行為」。依據當時英國法律，王爾德被判有罪，需在瑞丁和本頓維爾監獄服兩年勞役。這兩年間，他在獄中寫下詩作《瑞丁監獄之歌》和書信集《深淵書簡》。王爾德的妻子和兩個孩子在他入獄期間改姓遷居義大利，原本社交圈和文壇的朋友也都對他避之唯恐不及。在他落難時，僅有名劇作家蕭伯納 (George Bernard Shaw) 和少數幾位至交仍願意出面相挺。

經歷兩年苦牢生活後，王爾德對英國再無留戀。他在一八九七年前往巴黎，以聖經中受亂箭穿身而死的殉道者聖賽巴斯提安為靈感，化名賽巴斯提安‧梅爾摩斯 (Sebastian Melmoth) 隱居當地。出獄後的王爾德已風光不再，原本有意重修舊好的道格拉斯也體認到王爾德此時早已今非昔比。他曾說：「如果你不再是那個高高在上的王爾德，那一切都不再有趣。」隱居巴黎的這段時期，不時遇見的英國同鄉和他在風光時結識的法國友人更加深了王爾德的失意。

一九〇〇年，窮困潦倒又病危的王爾德在他的好友、而且曾是他的情人羅伯特‧羅斯 (Robert Ross) 的協助下，於臨死前受洗為天主教徒。十一月三十日，王爾德因腦膜炎病逝於巴黎的阿爾薩斯旅館 (Hôtel d'Alsace)，得年僅四十六歲。對於自己困居其中的這座破爛旅館，追求完美的他死前仍不改其幽默個性地說：「這醜壁紙和我正打得你死我活，我們當中總有一個得先走。」臨終時只有羅斯與另一位作家朋友瑞吉納‧透納 (Reginald Turner) 陪在身邊。羅斯是王爾德第一個同性情人，兩人相差十五歲；儘管王爾德後來情繫道格拉斯，但羅斯此生始終愛慕王爾德，並多方給予協助。王爾德死後遷葬於巴黎的拉榭斯神父墓園 (Cimetière du Père-Lachaise)，墓地按照他在詩集《斯芬克斯》中的意象，由藝術家艾普斯坦 (Jacob Epstein) 雕成一座帶有翅膀的人面獅身像。而羅斯在十八年後過世時，骨灰也依其遺願和王爾德合葬在此。

王爾德生前厭惡當時英國社會的虛偽道德觀，要用藝術的「美」對抗現實中的「醜」。他追求藝術形式之美，相信藝術唯有透過風格才能不朽；他不僅在服裝、語言和行為上創造出絢爛多彩的審美形式，也將之投射在自己的文學作品裡。天賦和自信過人的王爾德後半生雖然窮困潦倒，但他的熠熠才氣和成就依然讓他成為備受後世擁戴的作家。一九九八年，在王爾德孫子墨林‧荷蘭德 (Merlin Holland) 及曾孫的見證下，一座由英國當代雕塑家瑪姬‧漢柏琳 (Maggie Hambling) 創作的紀念雕像在倫敦特拉法爾加 (Trafalgar) 廣場附近立起。在遭受詆毀將近百年後，英國社會終於讓他得到應有的榮譽。這座雕像旁刻有王爾德常被世人引用的語句：「We are all in the gutter, but some of us are looking at the stars.——我們都在陰溝裡，但仍有人仰望星空。」

掃描此處,看一段電影《Paris, Je t'aime》中,以王爾德和拉榭斯神父墓園為創作靈感的五分鐘短片。

I

On Man and Woman

輯一・男與女

Men become old,
but they never become good.

男人會變老，但永遠不學好。

溫夫人的扇子
Lady Windermere's Fan

A man who moralizes is usually a hypocrite, and a woman who moralizes is invariably plain.

愛說教的男人通常偽善，愛說教的女人必定平庸。

溫夫人的扇子
Lady Windermere's Fan

Rich bachelors should be heavily taxed. It is not fair that some men should be happier than others.

富有的單身漢應該課以重稅。
有些男人可比別人快活，這並不公平。

對話

In Conversation

Women are meant to be loved,
not to be understood.

女人是用來疼愛，
不是用來理解的。

沒有祕密的斯芬克斯
The Sphinx Without a Secret

Men are horribly tedious when they are good husbands,
and abominably conceited when they are not.

當好丈夫的男人無聊至極，
不是好丈夫的男人則是極端高傲自滿。

無足輕重的女人
A Woman of No Importance

Crying is the refuge of plain women but the ruin of pretty ones.

眼淚是平庸女人的庇護所，
卻是美女的致命傷。

溫夫人的扇子
Lady Windermere's Fan

When a man acts he is a puppet.
When he describes he is a poet.

男人動靜舉止時是個傀儡，說話陳述時則成了詩人。

身為藝術家的評論者

The Critic as Artist

A bad man is the sort of man who admires innocence,
and a bad woman is the sort of woman a man never gets tired of.

壞男人懂得欣賞純真，壞女人則讓男人永不嫌膩。

無足輕重的女人
A Woman of No Importance

Between men and women there is no friendship possible.
There is passion, enmity, worship, love, but no friendship.

男女之間絕無純友誼。
有熱情、仇恨、崇拜、愛意，就是沒有友誼。

溫夫人的扇子
Lady Windermere's Fan

Good looks are a snare that every sensible man would like to be caught in.

美貌是所有理性男人皆願意掉入的陷阱。

不可兒戲
The Importance of Being Earnest

I don't think there is a woman in the world who would not be a little flattered if one made love to her.
It is that which makes women so irresistibly adorable.

我認為世上沒有女人不愛聽甜言蜜語，
所以她們才可愛到難以抗拒。

無足輕重的女人
A Woman of No Importance

The husbands of very beautiful women belong to the criminal classes.

絕世美女的丈夫實屬犯罪階級。

格雷的畫像

The Picture of Dorian Gray

When a man is old enough to do wrong he should be old enough to do right also.

當一個男人成熟到可以做錯事，
他也應該成熟到能把事情做對。

無足輕重的女人
A Woman of No Importance

When men give up saying what is charming, they give up thinking what is charming.

當男人不再講一樣東西迷人，就表示他不再想什麼是迷人了。

溫夫人的扇子

Lady Windermere's Fan

One should never trust a woman who tells one her real age.
A woman who would tell one that, would tell one anything.

絕不能相信透露真實年齡的女人，這樣的女人什麼
事都會對別人坦言。

無足輕重的女人

A Woman of No Importance

I don't know that woman are always rewarded for being charming. I think they are usually punished for it!

我不知道女人總能因美貌而得到好處，倒覺得美貌通常會令她們受罪。

理想丈夫
An Ideal Husband

Gerald: It is very difficult to understand women, is it not?
Lord Illingworth:You should never try to understand them.
Women are pictures. Men are problems.

傑瑞德：女人很難懂，對吧？
伊林沃茲勳爵：你不該試著去懂女人。女人是幅畫，
男人則是問題。

無足輕重的女人
A Woman of No Importance

Women know life too late.

That is the difference between men and women.

女人對人生的透徹來得晚，這就是男女之間的差異。

無足輕重的女人

A Woman of No Importance

Never trust a woman who wears mauve,
whatever her age may be,
or a woman over thirty-five who is fond of pink ribbons.
It always means they have history.

千萬別相信把淡紫色穿上身的女人，
無論她多大年紀。
也切勿相信三十五歲以上還喜歡粉紅緞帶的女人，
這代表她們有段過去。

格雷的畫像
The Picture of Dorian Gray

She will never love you unless you are always at her heels;
women like to be bothered.

除非你緊追在後，否則她不會愛你；
女人喜歡你的打擾。

薇拉，那群虛無主義者

Vera, or The Nihilists

Plain women are always jealous of their husbands.
Beautiful women never have time.
They are always so occupied in being jealous of other people's husband.

平庸女人愛吃老公的醋，漂亮女人可沒這等閒功夫，她們總忙著吃別人老公的醋。

無足輕重的女人
A Woman of No Importance

American girls are as clever at concealing their parents as
English women are at concealing their past.

美國女孩很精明，她們瞞著自己父母的本事，
就跟英國女人隱藏自己的過去一樣厲害。

格雷的畫像
The Picture of Dorian Gray

The one charm of the past is that it is past.
But women never know when the curtain has fallen.

過去的迷人之處就在事情已成往事，
但女人從不知這戲幕是何時落下的。

格雷的畫像
The Picture of Dorian Gray

She looks like a woman with a past.
Most pretty women do.

她看起來像是個有段過去的女人，
美女多半皆然。

理想丈夫
An Ideal Husband

Women are never disarmed by compliments.
Men always are. That is the difference between sexes.

恭維一向無法軟化女人，對男人倒是屢試不爽，
這就是男女之別。

An Ideal Husband
理想丈夫

It is only very ugly or very beautiful women who ever hide their faces.

唯有驚世醜女或絕世美女才會遮掩自己的面容。

The Duchess of Padua
帕都瓦公爵夫人

There is only one real tragedy in a woman's life.
The fact that her past is always her lover,
and her future invariably her husband.

女人一生只有一個真正的悲劇。
那就是她的過去屬於情人，未來只能屬於丈夫。

理想丈夫
An Ideal Husband

I prefer women with a past.

They are always so damned amusing to talk to.

我喜歡有段過去的女人，

跟她們交談總有說不出的樂趣。

溫夫人的扇子

Lady Windermere's Fan

Always!
That is a dreadful word. It makes me shudder when I hear it.
Women are so fond of using it.
They spoil every romance by trying to make it last forever.
It is a meaningless word too.
The only difference between a caprice and a lifelong passion is
that the caprice lasts a little longer.

永遠！
這兩個字多可怕，每次聽見都讓我渾身顫抖，
偏偏女人很愛掛在嘴邊。
她們想要愛情永恆，因此壞了每一段情。
這兩個字也毫無意義，
任性和一輩子的熱情唯一的差別，
就是任性還比熱情持久一些。

格雷的畫像
The Picture of Dorian Gray

The Book of Life begins with a man and woman in a garden.
It ends with Revelations.

生命之書從伊甸園裡的一男一女開始，
以《啟示錄》結束。

無足輕重的女人
A Woman of No Importance

Lady Stutfield:

Ah! The world was made for man and not for women.

Mrs. Allonby:

Oh, don't say that, Lady Stutfield.

We have a much better time than they have. There are far more things forbidden to us than are forbidden to them.

31

史塔特菲爾德女士：

這世界根本是為男人、而非女人打造的。

阿隆比夫人：

噢，妳可別這麼說。

我們女人的日子過得可比男人好，

我們被禁止的事情比他們的多太多了。

無足輕重的女人

A Woman of No Importance

We women, as someone says,
love with the ears,
just as you men love with eyes,
if you ever love at all.

就像有人說的，
我們女人用耳朵談戀愛，
你們男人則是用眼睛——
如果你們真的會愛的話。

格雷的畫像

The Picture of Dorian Gray

The strength of women comes from the fact that psychology
cannot explain us.
Men can be analysed, women...merely adored.

女人的力量來自於心理學無法解釋我們女人。
男人可被分析，而女人只能被疼愛。

理想丈夫
An Ideal Husband

If a woman wants to hold a man,
she has merely to appeal to what is worst in him...

女人若要拴住男人，
只要讓自己被他最糟糕的缺點吸引即可。

溫夫人的扇子
Lady Windermere's Fan

We made gods of men and they leave us.
Others make brutes of them and they fawn and are faithful.

我們把男人當成神，他們卻棄我們而去；
有些人把男人當畜生，他們反倒搖尾乞憐，
而且忠心耿耿。

溫夫人的扇子
Lady Windermere's Fan

I sometimes think that God in creating man,
somewhat overestimated His ability.

我有時候會想，
上帝在造人時，
似乎高估了祂自己的能力。

對話

In Conversation

On Marriage and Love

輯二・婚姻與愛情

All women become like their mothers.
That is their tragedy.
No man does. That's his.

所有的女人都會變得像自己的母親，
這是她們的悲劇。
男人則否，這是他們的悲劇。

不可兒戲

The Importance of Being Earnest

Men marry because they are tired;
women because they are curious;
both are disappointed.

男人結婚是因為倦了，
女人是因為好奇，
結果雙方皆大失所望。

格雷的畫像
The Picture of Dorian Gray

The real drawback to marriage is that it makes one selfish.
And unselfish people are colorless.

婚姻真實的缺點就是會讓人變得自私，
但無私的人則是平淡無趣。

格雷的畫像
The Picture of Dorian Gray

The happiness of a married man depends on the people he has not married.

已婚男人的幸福端看他沒娶到誰。

無足輕重的女人

A Woman of No Importance

If we men married the women we deserved,
we should have a very bad time of it.

我們男人要是娶了應得的女人，
日子可就難過了。

理想丈夫
An Ideal Husband

Twenty years of romance make a woman look like a ruin; but twenty years of marriage make her look like a public building.

二十年的愛情讓女人猶如一片斷垣殘壁，但二十年的婚姻則讓她好似一棟公共建築。

無足輕重的女人

A Woman of No Importance

In married life affection comes when people thoroughly dislike
each other.

婚姻生活中，當夫妻徹底嫌惡彼此時，
就是愛意降臨之際。

理想丈夫
An Ideal Husband

How marriage ruins a man!
It's as demoralizing as cigarettes, and far more expensive.

婚姻毀了男人！
婚姻跟香菸一樣傷風敗俗，而且比香菸貴多了。

溫夫人的扇子
Lady Windermere's Fan

The proper basis for marriage is mutual misunderstanding.

婚姻的合宜基礎應該建立在互相誤解上。

薩維爵士的罪行

Lord Arthur Savile's Crime

Nothing spoils a romance so much as a sense of humour in the woman — or the want of it in the man.

10

沒什麼比女人有幽默感 —— 或男人沒幽默感更破壞愛情的。

無足輕重的女人

A Woman of No Importance

The worst of having a romance of any kind is that it leaves one so unromantic.

在各種愛情中，
最糟糕的，
就是讓你變得不浪漫的那種。

格雷的畫像
The Picture of Dorian Gray

Any place you love is the world to you...
but love is not fashionable any more, the poets have killed it.
They wrote so much about it that nobody believes them,
and I am not surprised. True love suffers, and is silent.

你所愛的地方就是你的全世界⋯⋯
但「愛」已不再流行，都是詩人毀了愛之名。
詩人對愛的描寫已多到沒人願意相信他們，
這我一點兒也不詫異。
真愛很辛苦，而且苦不堪言。

驕傲的爆竹
The Remarkable Rocket

Men always want to be a woman's first love.
That is their clumsy vanity.
Women have a more subtle instinct about things:
What they like is to be a man's last romance.

男人總希望自己是女人的初戀，
這是男人愚蠢的虛榮。
女人的本能比較幽微：
她們希望自己是男人的最後一段情。

無足輕重的女人
A Woman of No Importance

What a silly thing love is! It is not half as useful as logic,
for it does not prove anything and it is always telling one things
that are not going to happen
and making one believe things that are not true.

愛情真是愚昧！
根本沒有邏輯來得一半有用。
愛情無法證明什麼，
而且總是告訴世人不可能發生的事，
讓他們相信不真實。

夜鶯與玫瑰

The Nightingale and the Rose

A kiss may ruin a human's life.

一個吻可能會毀掉一個人的一生。

無足輕重的女人
A Woman of No Importance

A man can be happy with any woman as long as he does not love her.

只要是自己不愛的女人，男人都不會挑剔。

格雷的畫像

The Picture of Dorian Gray

When one is in love one begins by deceiving oneself,
and one always ends by deceiving others.
That is what the world calls a romance.

人以自欺展開戀情，最後總以欺人結束，
這就是世間所謂的愛情。

無足輕重的女人
A Woman of No Importance

Young men want to be faithful and are not;
old men want to be faithless and cannot.

年輕男人有心忠誠，卻不忠誠；
老男人有意不忠，卻辦不到。

格雷的畫像

The Picture of Dorian Gray

Those who are faithful know only the trivial side of love:
it is the faithless who know love's tragedies.

忠誠守信的人只認識愛情瑣碎的一面，背信忘義者
才是真正認識愛情悲劇的人。

格雷的畫像
The Picture of Dorian Gray

Pleasure hides love from us but pain reveals it in its essence.

歡愉遮藏了愛，
而痛苦卻在本質中掀示了愛的面目。

獄中書信

Letter in prison

Everyone is worthy of love, except him who thinks that he is.

人人都值得愛，除了自以為值得的那個人。

深淵書簡
De Profundis

One should always be in love.
That is the reason one should never marry.

人應該隨時沉浸愛河，這就是人不該結婚的理由。

無足輕重的女人
A Woman of No Importance

London is full of women who trust their husbands.
One can always recognize them.
They look so unhappy.

倫敦滿是信賴自己丈夫的女人。
這誰都認得出來，
因為她們無不愁容滿面。

溫夫人的扇子
Lady Windermere's Fan

When a woman marries again it is because she detested her first husband. When a man marries again, it is because he adored his first wife. Women try their luck; men risk theirs.

女人再婚，是因為她厭惡第一任丈夫。
男人再婚，是因為他鍾愛第一任妻子。
女人想碰運氣，而男人則賭上運氣。

格雷的畫像

The Picture of Dorian Gray

I don't love novels that ends happily.
They depress me so much.

我不喜歡結局皆大歡喜的小說，
這種小說讓我沮喪不已。

不可兒戲
The Importance of Being Earnest

I have always been of opinion that a man who desires to get
married should know either everything or nothing.

我一向認為，
渴望結婚的男人若非通曉世事，就是一無所知。

不可兒戲

The Importance of Being Earnest

Our husbands never appreciate anything in us.
We have to go to others for that.

我們的丈夫都不懂欣賞我們，我們可得另找他人來
欣賞才是。

理想丈夫
An Ideal Husband

I suppose that when a man has once loved a woman,
he will do anything for her, except continue to love her?

我認為，男人一旦愛上女人，
什麼事情都肯為她做——除了繼續愛她以外？

理想丈夫

An Ideal Husband

Marriage is the one subject on which all women agree and all
men disagree.

婚姻是個所有女人皆贊成、
但全數男人皆反對的議題。

婚姻手冊
An Handbook to Marriage

More marriages are ruined nowadays by the common sense of the husband than anything else.

How can a woman be expected to be happy with a man who insists on treating her as if she were perfectly rational being?

這年頭，婚姻被為夫之道給毀掉的比什麼都來得多。
你怎能期望一直被丈夫當成絕對理性的人來對待的
女人能快樂呢？

無足輕重的女人

A Woman of No Importance

On Art and Fashion

輯三・藝術與時尚

All Art is immoral.

For emotion for the sake of emotion is the aim of art,

and emotion for the sake of action is the aim of life.

所有藝術都不道德。

為了情感而表達情感是藝術的目的，為了行動而表
達的情感則是人生的目的。

身為藝術家的評論者

The Critic as Artist

We live in an age when men treat art as if it were meant to be a form of autobiography.

我們生存的年代，把藝術當成一種自傳。

格雷的畫像

The Picture of Dorian Gray

The artist is a man who believes in himself,
because he is absolutely himself.

藝術家是相信自己的人，因為他完全自我。

社會主義下的靈魂
The Soul of Man Under Socialism

Bad artists always admire each other's work. They call it being largeminded and free from prejudice. But a truly great artist cannot conceive of life being shown or beauty fashioned, under any conditions other than those he has selected.

蹩腳的藝術家總會惺惺相惜，他們說這叫心胸寬大跟不存偏見。
但真正偉大的藝術家無法想像任何迥異於以自己選擇的方式所表現的人生或形塑的美。

身為藝術家的評論者
The Critics as Artist

No great artist ever sees things as they really are.
If he did he would cease to be an artist.

偉大藝術家眼中的事物向來不是原貌。
要是只見原貌,他就不再是藝術家了。

謊言的衰頹
The Decay of Lying

There are two ways of disliking art...
One is to dislike it. The other is to like it rationally.

討厭藝術的方法有兩種……
一種是憎惡藝術，另一種則是理性地喜歡藝術。

身為藝術家的評論者

The Critic as Artist

Popularity is the crown of laurel which the world puts on bad art. Whatever is popular is wrong.

流行是世界為劣等藝術加冕的桂冠，
流行的東西都有問題。

給藝術學生的一堂課
Lecture to Art Students

...the greatest superiority of France over England is that in
France every bourgeois wants to be an artist,
whereas in England every artist wants to be bourgeois.

對於英國，法國最大的優越感，
就是每個中產階級法國人都想當藝術家，
而每個英國藝術家則都想當中產階級。

對話

In Conversation

One touch of Nature may make the whole world kin,
but two touches of Nature will destroy any work of Art.

增添一點自然能讓世界可親，
但再多一點便會毀掉任何藝術作品。

謊言的衰頹
The Decay of Lying

Philosophy may teach us to bear with equanimity the misfortunes of our neighbours, and science resolve the moral sense into a secretion of sugar, but art is what makes the life of each citizen a sacrament.

哲學教我們安之泰若地接受鄰居的不幸，
科學則以醣類分泌解釋道德感，
但藝術則讓人民的生活成為聖禮。

在美國的演講

A Lecture in America

It is the spectator, and not life,
that art really mirrors.

藝術真正反映的不是人生，
而是觀者。

格雷的畫像
The Picture of Dorian Gray

We live in an age that reads too much to be wise,
and thinks too much to be beautiful.

我們這年代的人書讀得太多而不聰明，
想得太多而不美麗。

格雷的畫像

The Picture of Dorian Gray

If a man treats life artistically,
his brain is in his heart.

一個人若以藝術角度看待人生，
那他就是用心思考。

格雷的畫像

The Picture of Dorian Gray

The books that the world calls immoral books are books that show the world its own shame.

這世界所稱的敗德之書，
就是向這世界坦露其羞恥之處的作品。

格雷的畫像

The Picture of Dorian Gray

Anybody can write a three-volumed novel. It merely requires a complete ignorance of both life and literature.

只要完全無視人生和文學，
誰都寫得出三大卷的小說。

身為藝術家的評論者
The Critic as Artist

When the public say a work is grossly unintelligible, they mean that the artist has said or made a beautiful thing that is new; when they describe a work as grossly immoral, they mean that the artist has said or made a beautiful thing that is true.

當大眾評論一部作品莫名其妙，
意思是藝術家創造了嶄新的美；
當大眾形容一部作品道德淪喪，
意思是藝術家打造出真實的美。

社會主義下的靈魂
The Soul of Man Under Socialism

Poets know how useful passion is for publication.
Nowadays a broken heart will run to many editions.

詩人知道激情對出版多有幫助，
如今一顆破碎的心能反覆再版。

格雷的畫像
The Picture of Dorian Gray

The typewriting machine, when played with expression,
is not more annoying than the piano when played by a sister or
near relations

打字機要是敲得有感情，
並不比你的姊妹或親戚彈奏鋼琴來得擾人。

對話

In Conversation

...if one plays good music people don't listen, and if one plays bad music people don't talk.

演奏好的音樂沒人聽，演奏壞的音樂沒人討論。

不可兒戲
The Importance of Being Earnest

Musical people are so absurdly unreasonable.
They always want to be perfectly dumb at the very moment when one is longing to be absolutely deaf.

音樂家荒謬得不可理喻，每當有人巴不得聾了耳朵，
音樂家當下總想裝傻。

理想丈夫
An Ideal Husband

I like Wagner's music better than anybody's.
It is so loud that one can talk the whole time without people
hearing what one says.

我最喜歡華格納的音樂，
他的音樂吵到就算有人講話，旁人也聽不見。

格雷的畫像
The Picture of Dorian Gray

The discovery of America was the beginning of the death of art.

美國的發現就是藝術之死的開始。

對話

In Conversation

Many American ladies on leaving their native land adopt an appearance of chronic ill-health,
under the impression that it is a form of European refinement.

許多離開祖國的美國女人以慢性病容裝扮自己，
以為這就是高貴的歐式風格。

坎特維家的鬼魂
The Canterville Ghost

It is only the shallow people who do not judge by appearances.

唯有膚淺的人才不以貌取人。

格雷的畫像

The Picture of Dorian Gray

With an evening coat and a white tie, anybody, even a stock-broker, can gain a reputation for being civilized.

穿上燕尾服和白領結，任誰都是人模人樣，
就連證券交易員也不例外。

格雷的畫像
The Picture of Dorian Gray

A really well-made buttonhole is the only link between Art and Nature.

製作精良的鈕釦眼是藝術與自然間的唯一連結。

給年輕人的格言與哲學

Phrases and Philosophies for the Use of the Young

A well-tied tie is the first serious step in life.

一只繫得妥貼的領結，就是人生認真的第一步。

不可兒戲
The Importance of Being Earnest

She wore far too much rogue last night and not quite enough clothes. That is always a sigh of despair in a woman.

她昨晚濃妝艷抹，卻幾乎衣不蔽體，
這就是女人絕望的跡象。

理想丈夫
An Ideal Husband

Fashion is what one wears oneself.
What is unfashionable is what other people wear.

穿在自己身上的叫時尚，別人身上穿的就是不時尚。

理想丈夫
An Ideal Husband

One dagger will do more than a hundred epigrams.

一把匕首比百首諷刺短詩更具威力。

薇拉，那群虛無主義者

Vera, or The Nihilists

The telling of beautiful untrue things, is the proper aim of Art.

訴說美麗的不真實，就是藝術的確切目標。

謊言的衰頹
The Decay of Lying

Beauty has as many meanings as man has mood. Beauty is the symbol of symbols. Beauty reveals everything, because it expresses nothing. When it shows us itself it show us the whole fiery-coloured world.

美跟人類的情緒一樣，具有多種意思。
美是象徵中的象徵。
因為美不表達什麼，所以能揭露一切。
當美讓我們窺見其面貌，
也就讓我們看見火紅色的世界。

身為藝術家的評論者
The Critic as Artist

An idea that is not dangerous is unworthy of being called an idea at all.

毫不危險的想法根本不配稱為觀念。

身為藝術家的評論者

The Critic as Artist

A mirror will give back to one one's sorrow.
But Art is not a mirror, but crystal.

鏡子會反映出一個人的哀傷。
但藝術不是一面鏡子，而是水晶。

獄中書信

Letter in prison

To look at a thing is very different from seeing a thing.
One does not see anything until one sees its beauty.
Then and then only, does it come into existence.

觀看與領會是截然不同的兩回事。
除非悟出一樣東西的美，否則不算領會。
唯有如此，這樣東西才真正存在。

謊言的衰頹
The Decay of Lying

One should either be a work of art,
or wear a work of art.

一個人若不是一件藝術品，
身上就該穿戴一件藝術品。

給年輕人的格言與哲學

Phrases and Philosophies for the Use of the Young

It is always with the best intentions that the worst work is done.

最劣質的作品一向是在最好的意圖下完成的。

身為藝術家的評論者

The Critic as Artist

The tears that we shed at a play are a type of the exquisite sterile emotions that is the function of Art to awaken.
We weep but we are not wounded.
We grieve but our grief is not bitter.

我們看戲時落下的淚，正是藝術的功能，
用來喚醒冬眠的細膩感情。
我們感傷落淚，卻沒受傷。
我們悲痛，但悲傷卻不苦澀。

身為藝術家的評論者
The Critic as Artist

To fail and to die young is the only hope for a Scotsman who wishes to remain an artist.

一個蘇格蘭人若是還要當個畫家，
唯一希望就是一敗塗地，而且英年早逝。

對話

In Conversation

The English public, as a mass,
take no interest in a work of art until it is told that the work in
question is immoral.

為數眾多的英國大眾對藝術作品毫無興趣，
除非他們聽說這作品的道德大有問題。

對話

In Conversation

IV

On Sociality

輯四・談社交

Whenever people talk to me about the weather, I always feel certain that they mean something else.

每當有人跟我聊天氣，
我總覺得那肯定有弦外之音。

不可兒戲
The Importance of Being Earnest

There are only two kinds of people who are really fascinating—people who know absolutely everything and people who know absolutely nothing.

真正吸引他人的只有兩種人 ——
無所不知者，和一無所知者。

格雷的畫像

The Picture of Dorian Gray

Punctuality is the thief of time—
I am not punctual myself, but I do like punctuality in others.

準時是時間的偷兒 ——
我自己不準時，但我欣賞別人準時。

對話

In Conversation

When one pays a visit it is for the purpose of wasting other people's time, not one's own.

來客登門造訪的目的不是消磨他自己的時光，
而是在浪費別人的時間。

理想丈夫
An Ideal Husband

The most comfortable chair is the one I use myself when I have visitors.

最舒服的一張椅子，是客人來訪時我自己坐的那張。

理想丈夫

An Ideal Husband

Oh, I'm so glad you've come. There are hundred things I want not to say to you.

噢，我好高興你來了，我有一百件事不想告訴你。

對話

In Conversation

A publicist, nowadays is a man who bores the community with the details of the illegalities of his private life.

現代的公眾人物是拿自己私生活的非法細節讓大家
頻打哈欠的人。

筆、鉛筆與毒藥

Pen, Pencil and Poison.

A mask tells us more than a face.

8

面具傳達的訊息比面孔還多。

筆、鉛筆與毒藥

Pen, Pencil and Poison

There is only one thing in the world worse than being talked about, and that is not being talked about.

這世上只有一件事比成為他人討論焦點更慘，
那就是沒人討論。

格雷的畫像
The Picture of Dorian Gray

Murder is always a mistake... One should never do anything that one cannot talk about after dinner.

謀殺永遠是大錯特錯……
你永遠不該做出無法在茶餘飯後拿來閒聊的事。

格雷的畫像

The Picture of Dorian Gray

I usually say what I really think. A great mistake nowadays.
It makes one so liable to be misunderstood.

我通常會說真心話，
但這年頭說出真心話是個錯誤，
容易引起他人誤會。

理想丈夫
An Ideal Husband

Gossip is charming! History is merely gossip.
But scandal is gossip made tedious by morality.

八卦人人愛！
歷史不過就是八卦，而醜聞則是被道德搞得乏味的
八卦。

溫夫人的扇子
Lady Windermere's Fan

Lots of people act well but very few people talk well,
which shows that talking is much more the difficult thing of the
two, and much the finer thing also.

很多人舉止得宜，但話說得好的人可就少了，
這表示把話說好比較難，也更為細膩。

忠實的朋友

The Devoted Friend

I like talking to a brick wall,
it's the only thing in the world that never contradicts me.

我喜歡跟磚牆說話，
那是世上唯一不會反駁我的東西。

溫夫人的扇子
Lady Windermere's Fan

Conversation should touch everything but should concentrate itself on nothing.

對話應當面面俱到，無所不談，但又不可深談。

身為藝術家的評論者

The Critic as Artist

I hate people who talk about themselves, as you do, when one wants to talk about oneself, as I do.

像我這種想聊自己的人，討厭你這種愛聊自己的人。

驕傲的爆竹

The Remarkable Rocket

When people talk to us about others they are usually dull. When they talk to us about themselves they are nearly always interesting, and if one could shut them up, when they become wearisome, as easily as one can shut up a book of which one has grown wearied, they would be perfect absolutely.

道人長短的人通常乏味。
暢聊自己的人幾乎向來有趣。
要是他們懂得在自己令人疲乏時閉嘴，
就像一本書讀得厭倦時能輕易闔上，
那他們就絕對完美。

身為藝術家的評論者
The Critic as Artist

When people agree with me I always feel that I must be wrong.

每當有人同意我的說法，我總覺得自己肯定是錯了。

身為藝術家的評論者

The Critic as Artist

Don't be conceited about your bad qualities.
You may lose them as you grow old.

不要對自己的缺點太自滿，你長大後缺點可能就消失了。

無足輕重的女人

A Woman of No Importance

To make a good salad is to be a brilliant diplomatist—
the problem is entirely the same in both cases.
To know exactly how much oil one must put with one's vinegar.

製作一碗美味沙拉，就像是當一名圓滑的外交高手
—— 這兩者的問題完全相同，都是要明白該在醋裡
添上多少油。

薇拉，那些虛無主義者
Vera, or the Nihilists

Laughter is not at all a bad beginning for a friendship, and it is far the best ending for one.

以笑聲開始友情絕非壞事，
而友誼以笑聲結束則絕對是善終。

格雷的畫像

The Picture of Dorian Gray

What is interesting about the people in good society is the
mask that each one of them wears,
not the reality that lies behind the mask.

上流社會的有趣之處，在於每個人所戴的面具，
而不是面具背後的真實。

謊言的衰頹

The Decay of Lying

I love London Society! I think it has immensely improved.
It is entirely composed now of beautiful idiots and brilliant
lunatics. Just what Society should be.

我愛倫敦上流社會！
我認為倫敦上流社會已經大幅進步了，
現在完全是美麗的蠢蛋和聰明瘋子的天下，
上流社會就該如此。

理想丈夫
An Ideal Husband

Thirty-five is a very attractive age.
London society is full of women of the very highest birth who have, of their own free choice, remained thirty-five for years.

三十五是非常有魅力的年紀。
倫敦上流社會滿是出身高貴的女人，她們多年來都選擇自願保持在三十五歲。

不可兒戲
The Importance of Being Earnest

London is full of fogs—and serious people.
Whether the fogs produce the serious people or whether,
the serious people produce the fogs,
I don't know, but the whole thing rather gets on my nerves.

倫敦充滿霧氣和正經八百的人。
我不知道是霧氣讓人正經八百，
還是正經八百的人招來霧氣，但這件事讓我很煩惱。

溫夫人的扇子
Lady Windermere's Fan.

England will never be civilized until she has added Utopia to her dominions.

英格蘭得把烏托邦納入國家版圖，
才能走向文明。

身為藝術家的評論者
The Critic As Artist

I don't desire to change anything in England except the weather.

我不想改變英格蘭任何事物，
除了天氣。

格雷的畫像
The Picture of Dorian Gray

We have really everything in common with America nowadays,
except, of course, language.

28

這年頭我們和美國幾乎什麼都雷同，
當然了，除了語言之外。

坎特維家的鬼魂

The Canterville Ghost

It is a very dangerous thing to listen.
If one listens one may be convinced;
and a man who allows himself to be convinced by an argument
is a thoroughly unreasonable person.

聆聽是件十分危險的事。
你要是聆聽，就可能被說服，
而讓自己被爭論說服的男人根本荒謬至極。

理想丈夫

An Ideal Husband

I dislike arguments of any kind.
They are always vulgar, and often convincing.

我厭惡任何形式的爭論。
爭論向來粗俗，
而且通常極具說服力。

不可兒戲
The Importance of Being Earnest

To be natural is such a very difficult pose to keep.

自然是最難維持的姿態。

理想丈夫
An Ideal Husband

Nothing looks so like innocence as an indiscretion.

沒有什麼可比魯莽更顯無辜。

薩維爵士的罪行

Lord Arthur Savile's Crime

The basis of every scandal is an immoral certainty.

每一椿醜聞的基礎都建立在不道德的必然上。

格雷的畫像

The Picture of Dorian Gray

I love scandals about other people,
but scandals about myself don't interest me.
They have not got the charm of novelty.

我喜歡別人的醜聞，但對自己的可就沒興趣了。
自己的醜聞當中就是少了點新奇的吸引力。

格雷的畫像
The Picture of Dorian Gray

In modern life nothing produces such an effect as a good platitude. It makes the whole world kin.

現代生活中，沒什麼可比一句好的陳腔濫調，
更能營造出四海一家親的效果。

理想丈夫
An Ideal Husband

I like looking at geniuses, and listening to beautiful people.

我喜歡眼看著天才，但耳聽著俊美的人說話。

理想丈夫

An Ideal Husband

Beauty, real beauty,
ends where an intellectual expression begins.
Intellect is in itself a mode of exaggeration and destroys the
harmony of any face.

機智的表情一旦開始，真正的美就隨即隕落。
才智本身即是一種誇張，會破壞任何臉蛋的和諧。

格雷的畫像
The Picture of Dorian Gray

Serious is the only refuge of the shallow!

嚴肅是淺薄的唯一庇護所！

對話

In Conversation

I love political parties.
They are the only place left to us where people don't talk politics.

我愛政黨。
政黨是眾人唯一不談論政治的地方。

理想丈夫
An Ideal Husband

I may have said the same thing before... But my explanation,
I am sure, will always be different.

同一件事我先前可能說過了，
不過，我確信我的解釋一直會不同。

對話

In Conversation

On Human Nature

輯五・論人性

Man can believe the impossible, but man can never believe the improbable.

人能夠相信不可能，卻從不相信機會渺茫。

謊言的衰頹
The Decay of Lying

One can always be kind to people about whom one cares nothing.

人總能對自己毫不在乎的人和善相待。

格雷的畫像

The Picture of Dorian Gray

It is absurd to divide people into good and bad.
People are whether charming or tedious.

把人區分為好與壞,著實荒謬。
人不是迷人就是乏味。

溫夫人的扇子
Lady Windermere's Fan

When people talk to us about others they are usually dull.
When they talk to us about themselves they are nearly always
interesting.

道人是非長短者通常枯燥乏味，
但當他談起自己時卻往往趣味橫生。

身為藝術家的評論者

The Critic as Artist

The more one analyses people,
the more all reasons for analysis disappear.
Sooner or later one comes to that dreadful universal thing
called human nature.

一個人越是去分析別人，就越失去分析的理由，
遲早會掉入那可怕、名曰「人性」的普遍境地。

謊言的衰頹
The Decay of Lying

The public have an insatiable curiosity to know everything, except what is worth knowing.

大眾對大小事都有無盡的求知慾 ——
除了真正值得知道的事情例外。

社會主義下的靈魂
The Soul of Man Under Socialism

I like persons better than principles and I like persons with no principles better than anything else in the world.

比起原則，我更喜歡人。
這世上我最愛的就是沒有原則的人。

格雷的畫像
The Picture of Dorian Gray

We are each our own devil, and we make this world our hell.

我們就是自己的惡魔，
而且你我讓這個世界成了自己的地獄。

帕都瓦公爵夫人
The Duchess of Padua

The only way to get rid of temptation is to yield to it.

拒絕誘惑的唯一方式，就是向它臣服。

格雷的畫像

The Picture of Dorian Gray

A red rose is not selfish because it wants to be a red rose.
It would be horribly selfish if it wanted all the flowers in the
garden to be both red and roses.

一朵想成為紅玫瑰的玫瑰並不自私，
要是它希望花園裡所有花朵都成為紅玫瑰，
那自私才真正駭人。

社會主義下的靈魂
The Soul of Man Under Socialism

Anybody can sympathize with the sufferings of a friend, but it requires a very fine nature to sympathize with a friend's success.

誰都能同情朋友的苦難，
但為朋友的成功開心卻要有好性情。

社會主義下的靈魂
The Soul of Man Under Socialism

I would sooner lose my best friend than my worst enemy. To have friends, you know, one need only be good-natured; but when a man has no enemy left there must be something mean about him.

我寧可失去朋友，也不要失去最難纏的敵人。
你要知道，一個人只要心地好，就會有朋友，
但一個人若毫無敵人，這人肯定刻薄。

薇拉，那些虛無主義者
Vera, or The Nihilists

Morality is simply the attitude we adopt to people whom we personally dislike.

道德不過是我們用來針對自己討厭的人的態度。

理想丈夫

An Ideal Husband

Man is least himself when he talks in his own person. Give him a mask, and he will tell you the truth.

以真面目示人時，一個人說的話最不像自己。
給他一副面具，他就會傾吐真相。

身為藝術家的評論者
The Critic as Artist

A truth ceases to be true when more than one person believes in it.

一件事實只要超過一個人相信，便不再是真相。

給年輕人的格言與哲學

Phrases and Philosophies for the Use of the Young

Experience is the name every one gives to their mistakes.

經驗是人人為自己的過錯冠上的美名。

溫夫人的扇子

Lady Windermere's Fan

A little sincerity is a dangerous thing, and a great deal of it is absolutely fatal.

一點真摯帶有危險，真摯過度就絕對致命。

身為藝術家的評論者
The Critic as Artist

To realize one's nature perfectly—that is what each of us is here for.

完全透悉自己的本性 —— 這是你我此生來走一遭的
目的。

格雷的畫像

The Picture of Dorian Gray

Ideals are dangerous things.
Realities are better.
They wound, but they're better.

理想是危險的東西，真實比較好。
真實會傷人，但比較好。

溫夫人的扇子
Lady Windermere's Fan

To be good, according to the vulgar standard of goodness,
is obviously quite easy.
It merely requires a certain amount of sordid terror,
a certain lack of imaginative thought,
and a certain low passion for middle-class respectability.

從庸俗的好標準來看，當好人顯然很簡單。
只需要一定程度的惹人厭、缺乏想像力，
和對中產階級的體面不太懷抱熱情即可。

身為藝術家的評論者
The Critic as Artist

If there was less sympathy in the world there would be less trouble in the world.

要是這世上少點同情心，這世界就不會有這麼多麻煩。

理想丈夫

An Ideal Husband

It must be remembered that while sympathy with joy intensifies the sum of joy in the world,

sympathy with pain does not really diminish the amount of pain. It may make man better able to endure evil,

but the evil remains.

切記，對快樂感同身受雖會增加世上的歡樂，
但對痛苦感同身受卻無法消弭痛苦。
雖然如此讓人更能忍受惡行，但惡行不會因此消失。

社會主義下的靈魂
The Soul of Man Under Socialism

It is only shallow people who require years to get rid of an emotion.
A man who is master of himself,
can end a sorrow as easily as he can invent a pleasure.

唯有淺薄的人需要用數年掙脫一種情感。
一個人當得了自己的主人，便可輕易終結哀傷，
輕易製造快樂。

格雷的畫像
The Picture of Dorian Gray

Moods don't last. It is their chief charm.

情緒不持久，這就是它主要的迷人之處。

無足輕重的女人

A Woman of No Importance

.

Whenever a man does a thoroughly stupid thing, it is always from the noblest of motives.

當一個人做出徹底的蠢事，那通常是出於最高尚的動機。

格雷的畫像

The Picture of Dorian Gray

Being natural is simply a pose, and the most irritating pose I know.

保持自然不過是一種姿態，而且是我所知最惹人厭的姿態。

格雷的畫像

The Picture of Dorian Gray

All influence is bad, but a good influence is the worst in the world.

所有影響皆屬惡性，但好影響則是世上最糟糕的。

無足輕重的女人

A Woman of No Importance

Moderation is a fatal thing. Enough is as bad as meal.
More than enough is as good as a feast.

節制要人命，「剛剛好」就跟粗食便飯一樣差勁；
超過剛剛好才算盛宴。

格雷的畫像

The Picture of Dorian Gray

Sin is a thing that writes itself across a man's face.
It cannot be concealed.

罪會自己寫在人的臉上，無處可藏。

格雷的畫像

The Picture of Dorian Gray

I can resist everything except temptation.

我什麼都抗拒得了，就是抗拒不了誘惑。

溫夫人的扇子

Lady Windermere's Fan

Wickedness is a myth invented by good people to account for the curious attractiveness of others.

「邪惡」是善良之人創造的神話,用來說明他人的奇妙吸引力。

給年輕人的格言與哲學

Phrases and Philosophies for the Use of the Young

The only difference between the saint and sinner is that every saint has a past, and every sinner has a future.

聖者與罪人唯一的不同處，
就是每位聖者都有段過去，而每個罪人都有段未來。

無足輕重的女人
A Woman of No Importance

Nobody ever commits a crime without doing something stupid.

犯罪的人必做蠢事。

格雷的畫像

The Picture of Dorian Gray

There is only one thing worse than injustice,
and that is justice without her sword in her hand.
When right is not might it is evil.

比不正義更可惡的只有一件事，
那就是正義女神的手上沒有持劍。
當權力少了力量，那就是惡。

對話

In Conversation

An inordinate passion for pleasure is the secret of remaining young.

縱情追求歡愉，就是保持年輕的祕訣。

薩維爵士的罪行

Lord Arthur Savile's Crime

What people call insincerity is simply a method by which we
can multiply our personalities.

世人所說的不真誠，不過是我們讓個性多元的方式
而已。

身為藝術家的評論者

The Critic as Artist

The things one feels absolutely certain about are never true.
That is the fatality of Faith, and the lesson of Romance.

人百分之百確信的事從來都不會是真的。
這是信仰的宿命，愛情的教訓。

格雷的畫像

The Picture of Dorian Gray

Society often forgives the criminal; it never forgives the dreamer.

社會通常會原諒罪犯，卻從不原諒夢想家。

身為藝術家的評論者

The Critic as Artist

The public is wonderfully tolerant.
It forgives everything except genius.

社會大眾真的包容心十足，他們什麼都可原諒，
唯獨不原諒天才。

身為藝術家的評論者
The Critic as Artist

Only the shallow know themselves.

唯有膚淺的人才懂自己。

給年輕人的格言與哲學

Phrases and Philosophies for the Use of the Young

On Life

輯六・看人生

No man is rich enough to buy back his past.

沒有人富有到能贖回過去。

理想丈夫

An Ideal Husband

Men who are trying to do something for the world, are always insufferable, when the world has done something for them, they are charming.

想為世界做點什麼的人通常讓人難以忍受。
當世界在他們身上做了點什麼時,他們則變得迷人。

對話

In Conversation

Everyone is born a king, and most people die in exile, like most kings.

人人出生時皆是國王，死時多半流亡在外，一如多數的君主。

無足輕重的女人

A Woman of No Importance

Life is much too important a thing ever to talk seriously about it.

人生太重要，
重要到不該嚴肅論之。

薇拉，那些虛無主義者
Vera, or The Nihilists

To live is the rarest thing in the world.
Most people exist, that is all.

世上罕有人真正活著，多數人只是存在，
如此而已。

社會主義下的靈魂
The Soul of Man Under Socialism

Life is never fair...
And perhaps it is a good thing for most of us that it is not.

人生向來不公平……
或許不公平對大部分人而言算是件好事。

理想丈夫
An Ideal Husband

I love acting.
It is so much real than life.

我喜愛演戲。
演戲比人生更加真實。

格雷的畫像

The Picture of Dorian Gray

One should absorb the colour of life, but one should never remember its details. Details are always vulgar.

人應該吸收人生的色彩，可是永遠都別記得細節。
細節通常庸俗。

格雷的畫像

The Picture of Dorian Gray

When the gods wish to punish us they answer our prayers.

當諸神想懲罰我們，就會回應我們的禱告。

理想丈夫
An Ideal Husband

The world is a stage, but the paly is badly cast.

世界是一座舞台，只是這齣戲選角不佳。

薩維爵士的罪行

Lord Arthur Savile's Crime

The world has always laughed at its own tragedies,
that being the only way in which it has been able to bear them.

這世界總是嘲笑自身的悲劇。
唯有如此，它才能承受這些悲劇。

無足輕重的女人
A Woman of No Importance

But the past is of no importance.
The present is of no importance.
It is with the future that we have to deal.
For the past is what man should not have been.
The present is what man ought not to be.
The future is what artists are.

過去不重要，現在也不重要，
我們應該面對的是未來。
因為過去是你我不該有過的過去，
現在是人們不該活在的現在。
未來才是藝術家的所在。

社會主義下的靈魂
The Soul of Man Under Socialism

In this world there are only two tragedies.
One is not getting what one wants and the other is getting it.

這世上只有兩種悲劇，一種是無法心想事成，
另一種是心想事成了。

溫夫人的扇子
Lady Windermere's Fan

I never travel without my diary.
One should always have something sensational to read in the train.

我旅行必帶上自己的日記。
在火車上應該要有精采的東西可讀。

不可兒戲
The Importance of Being Earnest

Actions are the first tragedy in life, words are the second.
Words are perhaps the worst. Words are merciless.

行動是人生的第一場悲劇，言語則是第二場。
言語或許最為可惡，它殘酷無情。

溫夫人的扇子
Lady Windermere's Fan

All ways end at the same point...
Disillusion.

16

所有道路都在同一點終結……
這個點就叫幻滅。

格雷的畫像
The Picture of Dorian Gray

It is much more difficult to talk about a thing than to do it.
In the sphere of actual life that is of course obvious.
Anybody can make history. Only a great man can write it.

談論一件事比去做更難，這在真實人生中已經很明顯。誰都可以創造歷史，但唯有偉大者能寫出歷史。

身為藝術家的評論者
The Critic as Artist

The old believe everything; the middle-aged suspect everything; the young know everything.

18

老年人無所不信；中年人無所不疑；
年輕人無所不知。

給年輕人的格言與哲學

Phrases and Philosophies for the Use of the Young

The soul is born old but grows young.
That is the comedy of life.
And the body is born young but grows old.
That is life's tragedy.

靈魂出生蒼老但逐日年輕，這是生命的喜劇。
肉體出生年輕卻日漸衰圮，這是生命的悲劇。

無足輕重的女人
A Woman of No Importance

It is personalities, not principles,
that move the age.

推動一個年代的是個性，
不是原則。

對話

In Conversation

It is a terrible thing for a man to find out suddenly that all his life he has been speaking nothing but the truth.

突然發現自己終此一生只講真話,對一個人來說是件很恐怖的事。

不可兒戲

The Importance of Being Earnest

What seem to us bitter trials are often blessings in disguise.

22

我們眼裡的苦澀艱難，通常是經過偽裝的祝福。

不可兒戲

The Importance of Being Earnest

Life is not complex. We are complex.
Life is simple, and the simple thing is the right thing.

生命並不複雜，複雜的是我們。
生命很簡單，簡單的事才是正確的。

獄中書信
Letter in prison

One should always be a little improbable.

人應該永遠保持一點荒謬。

給年輕人的格言與哲學

Phrases and Philosophies for the Use of the Youn

I am the only person in the world I should like to know
thoroughly; but I don't see any chance of it just at present.

我是我在這世上唯一應當透徹了解的人，
但我怎麼看都覺得不可能。

溫夫人的扇子
Lady Windermere's Fan

Pain, unlike pleasure, wears no mask.

疼痛不若歡愉，它不戴面具。

深淵書簡

De Profundis

"Too late now" are in art and life the most tragical words.

在藝術和人生上，
「如今已太遲」都是最悲慘的字詞。

書信

In Letter

Skepticism is the beginning of faith.

懷疑是信仰的開始。

格雷的畫像

The Picture of Dorian Gray

To get back one's youth,
one has merely to repeat one's follies.

要重返青春年少，
你只需重蹈自己的愚行即可。

格雷的畫像

The Picture of Dorian Gray

I wrote when I did not know life.
Now that I know the meaning of life, I have no more to write.

過去我不識人生，故我寫。
現在我領悟了人生意義，卻再也無可下筆。

對話

In Conversation

王爾德作品一覽

小說

《格雷的畫像》（*The Picture of Dorian Gray*，1891 年）

童話集

《快樂王子與其他故事》（*The Happy Prince and Other Tales*，1888 年）
《石榴屋》（*A House of Pomegranates*，1891 年）

短篇故事

《坎特維家的鬼魂》（*The Canterville Ghost*）
《沒有祕密的斯芬克斯》（*The Sphinx Without a Secret*）
《模範百萬富翁》（*The Model Millionaire*）
《薩維爵士的罪行》（*The Arthur Savile's Crime*）

詩作

《詩集》（*Poems*，1881 年）
《斯芬克斯》（*Sphinx*，1894 年）
《瑞丁監獄之歌》（*The Ballad of Reading Gaol*，1898 年）

劇作

《薇拉，那群虛無主義者》（*Vera, or The Nihilists*，1880 年）
《溫夫人的扇子》（*Lady Windermere's Fan*，1892 年）
《帕都瓦公爵夫人》（*The Duchess of Padua*，1893 年）
《莎樂美》（*Salomé*，1893 年）
《無足輕重的女人》（*A Woman of No Importance*，1892 年。隔年首演）
《不可兒戲》（*The Importance of Being Earnest*，1895 年）
《理想丈夫》（*An Ideal Husband*，1895 年。）

其他著作

《社會主義下的靈魂》（*The Soul of Man Under Socialism*，1891 年。）
《深淵書簡》（*De Profundis*，1897 年。1905 年作者死後出版）
《筆、鉛筆和毒藥》（*Pen, Pencil and Poison*）
《身為藝術家的評論者》（*The Critic As Artist*）
《謊言的衰頹》（*The Decay of Lying*）

人生太重要，重要到不該嚴肅論之
王爾德妙語錄

作者｜奧斯卡‧王爾德 (Oscar Wilde)
譯者｜張家綺

主編｜林家任
行銷企劃總監｜蔡慧華
行銷企劃專員｜張意婷
排版｜宸遠彩藝
設計｜井十二設計研究室

出版｜八旗文化／遠足文化事業股份有限公司
發行｜遠足文化事業股份有限公司（讀書共和國出版集團）
地址｜新北市新店區民權路 108-2 號 9 樓
電話｜ 02.2218.1417
傳真｜ 02.2218.8057
客服專線｜ 0800.221.029
信箱｜ gusa0601@gmail.com

法律顧問｜華洋法律事務所 蘇文生律師
印刷｜通南彩色印刷股份有限公司

出版日期｜ 2019 年 05 月 平裝初版一刷
　　　　　 2023 年 06 月 平裝初版十刷
定價｜ 260 元

國家圖書館出版品預行編目 (CIP) 資料

人生太重要，重要到不該嚴肅
論之：王爾德妙語錄
奧斯卡‧王爾德 (Oscar Wilde)
著；張家綺譯 .-- 初版 .-- 新北市
八旗文化出版：遠足文化發行.
2019.05
240 面；13 × 21 公分

ISBN 978-957-8654-62-4（平裝）

873.4
108004777

掃描登入或臉書搜尋「八旗文化」